FC BARCELONA

by Jonathan Avise

An Imprint of Abdo Publishing
abdopublishing.com

EUROPE'S BEST
SOCCER CLUBS

abdopublishing.com

Published by Abdo Publishing, a division of ABDO, PO Box 398166, Minneapolis, Minnesota 55439.

SportsZone™ is a trademark and logo of Abdo Publishing.

Printed in the United States of America, North Mankato, Minnesota
062017
092017

Cover Photos: Bagu Blanco/BPI/Rex Features/AP Images, foreground; Keystone/AP Images, background
Interior Photos: Professional Sport/Popperfoto/Getty Images, 4; VI Images/Getty Images Sport/Getty Images, 7; Bob Thomas/Bob Thomas Sports Photography/Getty Images, 9, 10, 12; Staff/AFP/Getty Images, 14, 30; Bob Thomas/Popperfoto/Getty Images, 17; Mirrorpix/Newscom, 18; Manu Fernandez/AP Images, 21, 38, 41, 42; Dean Bertoncelj/Shutterstock Images, 22; Yuri Turkov/Shutterstock Images, 25; L. Gomez/AP Images, 27; Andres Kudacki/AP Images, 28; Cesar Rangel/AP Images, 33; Bernat Armangue/AP Images, 34; Alessandra Tarantino/AP Images, 37

Editor: Patrick Donnelly
Series Designer: Craig Hinton
Content Consultant: Paul Logothetis, European soccer reporter

Publisher's Cataloging-in-Publication Data

Names: Avise, Jonathan, author.
Title: FC Barcelona / by Jonathan Avise.
Description: Minneapolis, MN : Abdo Publishing, 2018. | Series: Europe's best soccer clubs | Includes bibliographical references and index.
Identifiers: LCCN 2016963087| ISBN 9781532111310 (lib. bdg.) | ISBN 9781680789164 (ebook)
Subjects: LCSH: Soccer--Europe--History--Juvenile literature. | Soccer teams--Europe--History--Juvenile literature. | Soccer--Europe--Records--Juvenile literature. | Futbol Club Barcelona (Soccer team)--Juvenile literature.
Classification: DDC 796.334--dc23
LC record available at http://lccn.loc.gov/2016963087

TABLE OF CONTENTS

Barcelona's Hristo Stoichkov makes a move against a Sampdoria defender.

CONQUERING EUROPE

By the early 1990s, FC Barcelona was the envy of much of the soccer world. It was a giant in the Spanish league. Barcelona had won multiple league and tournament titles. It had the undying support of the people of Catalonia, a unique region of the country that views itself as separate from the rest of Spain.

But one award was missing from the club's trophy case: the European Cup, the biggest prize in European club soccer.

Barcelona's fans were hopeful that was about to change. Manager Johan Cruyff, a former superstar for Barcelona and the

Dutch national team, had assembled what became known as the "Dream Team." It was a talented group of exciting attackers, artful midfielders, and steely defenders collected from across Europe.

Spanish stars Pep Guardiola and José Mari Bakero combined with Danish playmaker Michael Laudrup in the midfield. Dutch defender Ronald Koeman anchored the back line and devastated opponents with his free kicks. Bulgarian striker Hristo Stoichkov, meanwhile, was one of the world's most dangerous goal scorers. Together they made a powerful team.

On May 20, 1992, they gathered under the lights of London's famous Wembley Stadium. They were within one victory of capturing that elusive prize. The European club championship, now known as the UEFA Champions League, was on the line.

Coming Close

Since the competition began in 1955–56, Barcelona had several strong showings at the European Cup. But each time it fell short. In 1961 and 1986, Barcelona had advanced all the way to the final, only to lose.

Michael Laudrup avoids a Sampdoria defender's sliding tackle.

EUROPEAN SOCCER

The European soccer season is broken down into different levels of competition. It can be confusing to keep track of it all. Here's a handy guide to help you follow the action.

League Play

The 20 best teams in Spain play in La Liga. Teams play all league opponents twice each season for 38 total games. The three teams with the worst records are relegated—or sent down—to the second division, which sends its top three teams up to replace them the next season.

European Play

The top three teams in La Liga qualify for the group stage of the Union of European Football Associations (UEFA) Champions League. This annual tournament involves the best teams from the top leagues throughout Europe. The Champions League debuted in 1992. It replaced the European Cup, a similar tournament that began in 1955.

The fourth-place team enters Champions League play in the qualifying round. The next two teams from La Liga qualify for the UEFA Europa League. The Europa League is Europe's second-tier tournament. It runs in a similar manner to the Champions League but crowns its own winner. The Europa League debuted in 1971 as the UEFA Cup but was renamed in 2009.

Domestic Cups

Teams from the top four levels of Spanish soccer are eligible to play in the Copa del Rey, or King's Cup. Founded in 1903, the tournament is the oldest in Spain. The winning team automatically qualifies for the Europa League. It also faces the champion of La Liga in the *Supercopa de España* (Spanish Super Cup).

Barcelona supporters turned out in full force at Wembley Stadium.

Even worse, archrival Real Madrid had won six European titles and become the most successful club in history along the way.

In 1992 Barcelona again found itself just one win away from ending its quest. But a talented Italian team, Sampdoria, stood in its way.

"Go out and enjoy it," Cruyff told his players in the dressing room before the game. Then they went out and battled as

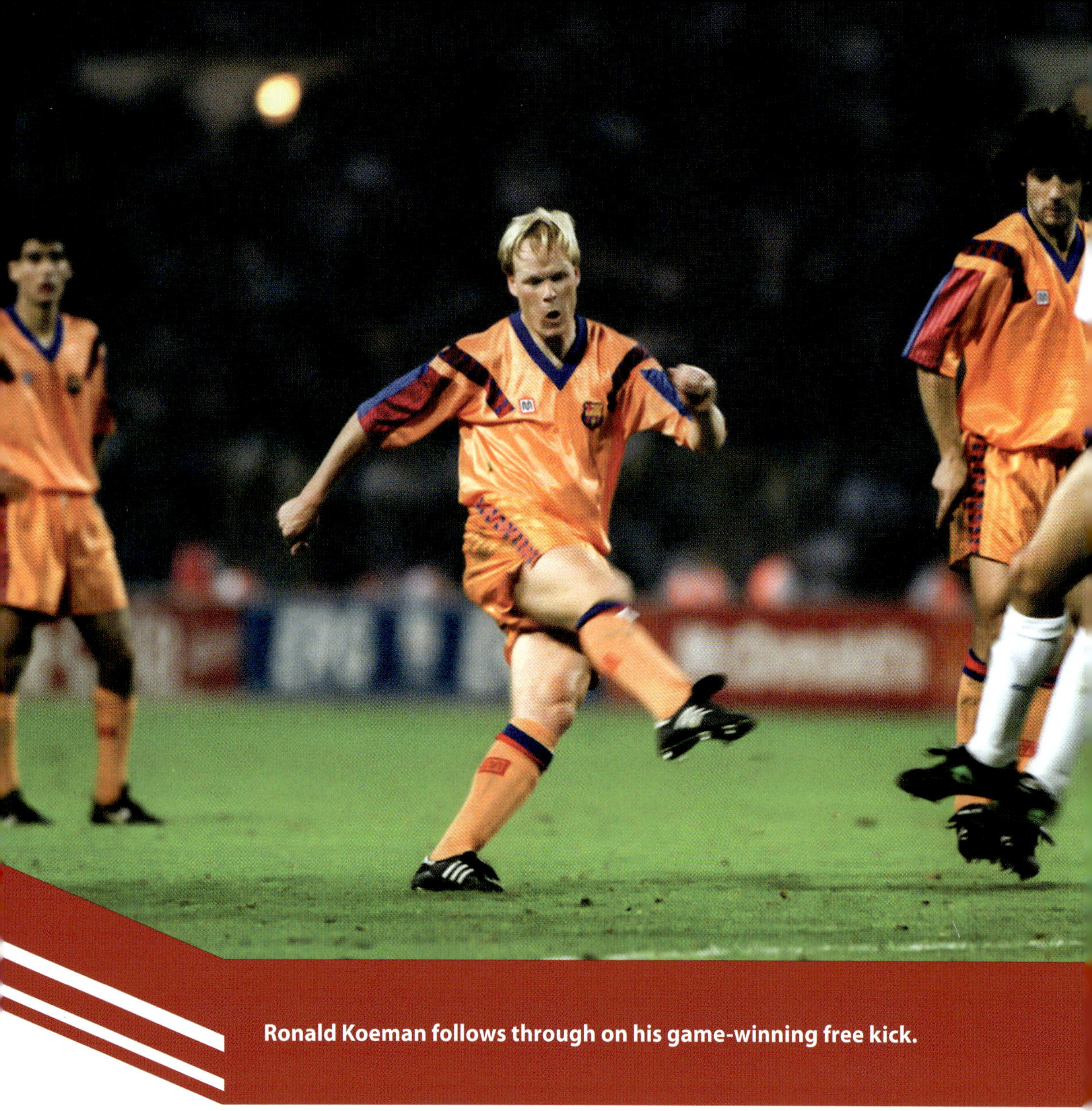

Ronald Koeman follows through on his game-winning free kick.

Sampdoria matched them step for step. For 90 minutes and into extra time, the Italian underdog hung tough. Neither side could break through the other's defense for a goal. Less than 10 minutes remained before penalty kicks would decide a winner.

The *blaugrana*, so nicknamed because of their traditional blue and garnet shirts, poked and prodded the sturdy Sampdoria defense. They were desperate for a goal.

Breaking Through

Barcelona's moment finally arrived with a free kick just beyond the penalty area in the 112th minute. Koeman, despite being a central defender, scored an amazing 102 goals in his Barcelona career. He had a powerful right leg and a special knack for scoring from set pieces. With everyone in the huge stadium watching every movement, the big Dutchman stepped up before a wall of white Sampdoria shirts, swung his right leg, and changed FC Barcelona history forever.

FAST FACT

Even though it didn't win the European Cup until 1992, Barcelona quickly moved up the ranks of European club winners. Through 2016 only Real Madrid (11) and AC Milan (seven) had won more European Cups or Champions League titles. German giant Bayern Munich was tied with Barcelona as a five-time champion.

The ball rocketed toward the lower left corner of the goal. Sampdoria's keeper made a late dive to his right, but it was

too late. The ball found the back of the net. As Barcelona's fans roared, Koeman's teammates mobbed him in the corner of the field. Koeman, overcome by the emotions of the moment, buried his face in his hands.

The goal was all Barcelona needed. The 1–0 victory gave the club its first European Cup. The Dream Team went on to win four Spanish league titles in a row, ending in 1994. They set a new standard for Barcelona. Through 2016 the team had added four more European titles in the Champions League. The Dream Team's achievements set off the most successful era in the club's rich history.

These days, Barcelona stars such as Lionel Messi, Neymar, and Andres Iniesta entertain fans across the globe. But the Dream Team's victory that night in London marked the completion of a long journey to the top of the football world. It's a position Barcelona hasn't shown any signs of surrendering in the years since.

Barcelona players, having donned their traditional jerseys, celebrate their first European Cup title.

Hungarian striker Laszlo Kubala starred for Barcelona in the 1950s.

TURMOIL AND TITLES

The story of FC Barcelona began with a newspaper advertisement. In 1899 Swiss businessman Hans Gamper was looking for other soccer fans to help him start a club in Catalonia's capital. In a city park, he gathered a group of English, Swiss, Germans, and Catalans who responded to his ad. Together they founded Futbol Club (FC) Barcelona.

After some early struggles, Barcelona found its stride and began to have success playing against other clubs in the region. In 1928 Barcelona helped form Spain's professional league, La Liga. Success came fast in the new Spanish league.

Barcelona—or "Barca" (BAR-suh) as its fans often call the club—captured five early league championships.

Soon, political turmoil spread across Spain, leading to civil war. Barcelona found itself stuck in the middle of the unrest.

Regional Rebels

Catalonia's language, culture, and history are distinct from the rest of Spain. This meant it was viewed with suspicion by the country's dictator, General Francisco Franco. He banned many signs and symbols of Catalan culture throughout the country. FC Barcelona had to remove the Catalan flag from its club badge. And it was renamed *Club de Fútbol (CF) Barcelona*, the Spanish version of its name. Those changes remained in place until the mid-1970s, when Franco's reign ended.

Despite those obstacles, the club held strong. Playing under its new temporary name, CF Barcelona won La Liga three times between 1945 and 1949. Then a powerful Hungarian refugee helped it again rise to the top. Laszlo Kubala was an intimidating and muscular 5-foot-9-inch forward. He became the club's first superstar.

A soccer game at Camp Les Corts in Barcelona in the 1920s

With Kubala, Barcelona became the dominant team in Spanish soccer. Its 1951–52 team won five trophies in a single season. In the Catalan language that feat is known as the *Cinc Copes*, or five cups. Another star player, Spanish attacking midfielder Luis Suárez, joined the team in 1955.

All that success had led to a problem. Barcelona's stadium, Camp Les Corts, was suddenly too small. More space was needed to fit the club's growing fan base.

So in 1957 Barcelona opened a new 93,000-seat stadium. Its name, which remains today, is the nickname supporters gave it as it was being constructed: *Camp Nou*, or New Ground. It is now Europe's largest soccer stadium, with room for more than 99,000 fans.

But little money remained after the construction of the Camp Nou, and Barcelona soon fell from its perch atop Spanish soccer. For the next decade, rival Real Madrid dominated Spain and Europe.

FAST FACT

The Camp Nou seats more than 99,000 fans. But at one time it was even larger. Following an expansion in 1982, the Camp Nou had room for a whopping 115,000 fans. Later improvements, though, eliminated standing areas in the stadium and shrunk its capacity.

Cruyff Arrives

A shaggy-haired forward from the Netherlands helped change that. Johan Cruyff was among the world's best soccer players in 1973 when he arrived in Barcelona. He had starred for Dutch club Ajax for nine seasons. His signing paid off right away. Barcelona had been fourth-from-last place in the league when Cruyff

Johan Cruyff changed Barcelona's fortunes when he arrived from the Netherlands in 1973.

played his first game during the 1973–74 season. From there, the club went on a furious run. It went 22 matches without losing and eventually captured the league championship.

The league victory snapped a long 14-year title drought. Along the way, Cruyff and Barcelona delivered a famous 5–0 defeat to Real Madrid. The win served notice to its old rival that Barcelona was back. Cruyff and his graceful attacking play helped start a revolution at Barca. With the best player in the world on its side, the club no longer thought of itself as second-best to its rival.

He continued to help the club win as its manager, too. Cruyff took over the Barcelona bench in 1988 and built a historic team. Barcelona's Dream Team won four straight La Liga championships in the early 1990s and captured its first European Cup.

Those victories helped pave the way for the most successful period in

FAST FACT

La Masia is FC Barcelona's famous youth academy. There the club trains young players in the same style of play as its top team. Many great players have come through La Masia, including Pep Guardiola, Lionel Messi, Andres Iniesta, and Xavi Hernandez.

Lionel Messi, *left*, and Andres Iniesta are two of Barcelona's modern stars.

Barcelona's history. International stars Lionel Messi, Ronaldinho, Deco, Samuel Eto'o, Andres Iniesta, Carles Puyol, and Xavi Hernandez drove Barcelona to new heights. In 2006 a pair of late goals helped Barcelona beat Arsenal 2–1 for its second European title. Three more Champions League titles followed between 2009 and 2015. Those wins were in addition to 10 more league titles won between 1997 and 2016.

FCB

FC Barcelona's crest is one of the most recognizable logos in sports.

MÉS QUE UN CLUB

Millions of soccer fans love to cheer their favorite team. But for Barcelona fans, its team means something more.

Més que un club. More than a club. That's FC Barcelona's motto, spelled out on a swath of seats at the famous Camp Nou. What does it mean?

Barcelona's fans do more than simply cheer for their team. They have a direct impact on the direction of the club. The team's 177,000 paid members actually own and operate the club. The members, called *socis*, elect the club president and have a say in how the club is run.

"Barcelona is not a business," said former club president Sandro Rosell. "It is a feeling."

Politics and Pride

Key to what makes Barcelona more than a club is its political history. Barcelona is located in Catalonia, a region in northeast Spain separated from France by the Pyrenees mountain range. There, FC Barcelona has often represented more than soccer. Supporting Barca has been a way to show pride in the region.

The club's crest is a prime example of its Catalan pride. It features a red cross, the symbol of Catalonia's patron saint, Saint Jordi, and the red and yellow stripes of the once-banned Catalan flag.

FAST FACT

Barca is one of the most supported soccer clubs in the world. In addition to its more than 170,000 *socis*, the club has 1,354 supporters clubs worldwide. It also has a massive following online. Barcelona's 148 million followers on social media is the most of any sports team in the world. It's also more than all of the 32 National Football League teams combined.

Following the Spanish Civil War (1936–1939), when the dictatorship of Francisco Franco banned expressions of Catalan

Barcelona's club motto is on display at the Camp Nou.

culture such as its language and flag, the only way for Catalonia to express itself was through its favorite soccer club and most famous institution. Citizens of Barcelona could not fly their flag or openly oppose the dictatorship. But cheering on Barca was another way to act defiantly.

Politics helped to spark another unique part of club lore. In 1943 Barcelona met Real Madrid in the two-game semifinal round of the Spanish league cup tournament. Barcelona was masterful in the first game at its home stadium, winning 3–0. The home fans were thrilled, loudly booing and whistling at the Madrid team.

But before the second game in the Spanish capital, Barcelona players received a surprise visit. The director of state security, who was responsible for arresting opponents of the dictatorship, appeared in their dressing room before the game. It's been alleged that he let the players know that Madrid should win.

Barcelona went on to lose the game 11–1. With that, the Barcelona-Real Madrid rivalry had truly begun.

El Clasico

For the better part of a century, the two richest soccer clubs in the world have been locked in the world's most intense sports rivalry. The dislike runs deep. But the unique rivalry is about much more than just soccer.

Barcelona and Madrid are the two largest cities in Spain. Their biggest soccer clubs are seen to represent their very different regions of the country, Catalonia and Castile. And they are seen to symbolize, too, support for a single Spanish state versus Catalan independence.

Barcelona's Johan Neeskens stares down Real Madrid's Paul Breitner in a 1975 edition of El Clasico.

The presence of Lionel Messi, *left*, and Cristiano Ronaldo brings even more international attention to El Clasico.

Barcelona and Real Madrid share the spotlight, compete for top signings, and fight for league and European championships. Their fan bases cheer their own team's wins and also the losses of their rival.

Their matchups on the field are known as *El Clasico*, which means "The Classic." Spanish soccer fans, no matter which teams they support, plan their schedules around it. And with so much on the line, it's often the most watched sporting event in the world, with more than 100 million people tuning in worldwide.

The feud reached new heights with the arrival of the two greatest players in the world. Lionel Messi had been a star for Barcelona for five years when Cristiano Ronaldo joined Real Madrid in 2009. Between them they won every Ballon d'Or (given to the world's top player) from 2008 to 2016, and their rivalry has contributed to the carnival atmosphere surrounding *El Clasico*.

A few players have made the jump from one side of the divide to the other. Luis Figo is one of the most famous to swap shirts. The Portuguese midfielder moved from Barcelona to Real Madrid in 2000. Barcelona fans were not pleased. On a return visit to the Camp Nou in 2002, a spectator threw a pig's head on the field as Figo took a corner kick.

FAST FACT

El Clasico **is not FC Barcelona's only heated contest each season. The club has a local rivalry with fellow Barcelona club Espanyol, known as** ***El derbi Barceloni*** **or the Barcelona Derby. Politics has contributed to the rivalry. Espanyol was formed in opposition to FC Barcelona and its Swiss founders. Barcelona fans viewed Espanyol as supporters of the dictatorship in Madrid. The rivalry has been rather one-sided in Barcelona's favor, but the hard feelings remain.**

Alfredo Di Stefano, *left*, watches as Laszlo Kubala juggles a ball before a practice in 1958.

STARS OF THE PAST

Barcelona saw players come and go in the first half of the 20th century as it fought to gain prominence in the soccer world. The arrival of Laszlo Kubala from Hungary in 1951 gave the club its first true international superstar.

Agile and strong, Kubala helped start a golden age in the club's history. Josep Samitier, one of Barcelona's former coaches who scouted Kubala, called him "the foundation stone" for the club's future growth. Kubala brought with him countless goals and great skill. He escaped communist Hungary to play in Spain, and he quickly became Barcelona's best player. In 11 seasons with the club he scored 280 goals.

The club's first superstar, Kubala helped Barcelona win four league titles. He also played a part in five Copa del Rey titles. It was a run of success the club would not see again for 50 years.

El Flaco

Another European player headed south to make his mark on Spanish soccer in the 1970s. Johann Cruyff arrived in Barcelona from Amsterdam in 1973. He changed the club forever.

Known as *El Flaco*, or the Skinny One, Cruyff helped change the way Barcelona played with his intelligent and graceful style of soccer. The Dutch forward won the hearts of Barcelona fans with his statements of support for Catalonia. His 86 goals in six seasons didn't hurt, either.

Cruyff returned to manage the club in 1988 and again helped Barcelona find success. He led the team to four consecutive league titles and its first European Cup in 1992. His impact is still felt in Barcelona. He installed a quick-passing, skillful style of play that valued possession. Barcelona teams still use it today.

Few players had a bigger impact in a shorter time with Barcelona than Brazilian superstar Ronaldo.

"Johan Cruyff painted the chapel, and Barcelona coaches since merely restore or improve it," former Barcelona player and coach Pep Guardiola once said.

South American Stars

Barcelona has fielded a number of players who could have been considered the best in the world. Diego Maradona was one of those all-time greats who pulled on a Barcelona shirt. But his time in Catalonia wasn't his best. The Argentine battled illness

Ronaldinho had a memorable six-year run with Barcelona.

and injury in two seasons at the Nou Camp (1982–84). He left for Italy to play at Napoli, where he became known as the best player in the world.

Another South American legend had more success with Barcelona. Ronaldo Luiz Nazario, known around the world as simply Ronaldo, spent just one season in the *blaugrana* of FC Barcelona. But what a season it was. The Brazilian played 51 games for Barcelona in 1996–97. The 20-year-old scored an amazing 47 goals in those appearances. Like Maradona, he left for Italy, signing with Inter Milan the following summer.

Another Brazilian, Rivaldo, played five seasons in Barcelona. One of the best players in the world at the time, the attacking midfielder was at his best in Barcelona. He led the team to La Liga titles in his first two seasons, in 1998 and 1999. In his second season, Rivaldo was named World Player of the Year.

Few players have appeared to be having as much fun on a soccer field as Ronaldo de Assís Moreira. Better known as Ronaldinho, the Brazilian forward flashed his dazzling smile and talent during six seasons at the Camp Nou. He scored 94 goals in the blue and red of Barcelona. And he made jaws drop with his slick dribbling and stylish passes. He was so good he once earned a standing ovation from rival Real Madrid's supporters.

Ronaldinho was considered the best player in the world for a time. He helped lead Barcelona to its second European victory in the 2006 Champions League final.

Pep Leads the Way

Josep "Pep" Guardiola served as manager from 2008 to 2012 and led Barcelona to its most successful period in club history. It was a continuation of an already strong legacy.

Guardiola was a son of Catalonia, growing up near Barcelona. He rose through the club's youth ranks from the age of 13. In 1990 he took a place in the first team's midfield and led the team for the next decade.

Guardiola scored few goals, but he helped create many. He was a key cog in the Barcelona team. Guardiola was an expert passer with great vision and quick reactions. He directed the action on the field for the Barcelona team that won the club's first European Cup in 1992.

When he returned as manager, the club won two more Champions League titles and 14 of the 19 trophies for which it competed.

The beginning of his managing term overlapped with the end of another great player's career. Cameroonian Samuel Eto'o had a nose for the net during his time with Barcelona. Eto'o played in 232 games for Barcelona from 2004 to 2009. He scored 152 goals, putting him among the top scoring threats in

Barcelona players throw coach Pep Guardiola into the air to celebrate their 2009 Champions League title.

team history. He scored important goals, too. Eto'o netted one in both the 2006 and 2009 Champions League finals. Along with Ronaldinho, he helped create a nearly unstoppable duo that helped tilt the balance of league power away from Madrid.

LFP
FIFA
FCB
Qatar
Foundatio
10
bet3

No player has had more to celebrate in Barcelona than Lionel Messi.

CHAPTER 5

MODERN STARS

Pep Guardiola helped usher in a new generation of greatness as a player with the 1990s-era Dream Team. Then he led the team to even greater heights during his seven years as a manager. His teams won trophies and did so with an exciting playing style. Of course, it helped that he had several world-class players to direct.

No player was more important than Argentinean forward Lionel Messi. He stands only 5 feet 7 inches and was dismissed as too small, too weak, or too fragile as a youth player in Argentina. To say he put those fears to rest is an understatement.

Messi had not yet reached his 30th birthday when the 2016 season began, but he's considered by many the greatest player in history. He arrived at Barcelona at age 13 and tore through the club's youth ranks, making his debut with the top club when he was just 17. Within eight years he'd broken the club's all-time career scoring record. And in 2012 he scored 91 goals between his appearances with Barcelona and Argentina. That broke a 40-year-old record for most goals by a player in a calendar year.

Messi exudes skill and confidence. The forward is a magician with the ball at his feet, holding off much larger defenders and scoring at a furious pace. Through 2016 he had been awarded the Ballon d'Or five times.

Talented Teammates

But Messi doesn't do it by himself. He's gotten plenty of help from other elite players such as Brazilian defender Dani Alves, striker Luis Suárez from Uruguay, and homegrown hero Xavi Hernandez. It's been said that if Barcelona were a car, Xavi would be its engine. The midfield genius was born in nearby Terrassa and came up through Barcelona's La Masia youth

Xavi, *center*, scores a goal against La Liga opponent Sporting Gigon in 2012.

academy. Xavi joined the club at the age of 12 and grew up immersed in the Barcelona style of play. He anchored the Barcelona midfield from 1998 to 2015. With tremendous vision of the field, he sprayed passes across the field with accuracy. And he could win the ball back from opponents when Barcelona lost it.

The club record holder for appearances with 869, Xavi helped Barcelona win four Champions League titles and eight

Neymar celebrates a Barcelona goal on the back of teammate Dani Alves in 2015.

La Liga championships. He was also a key cog for the Spanish national teams that won Euro 2008, Euro 2012, and the 2010 World Cup.

Two-Way Threat

Other players succeed with flash. Andrés Iniesta has done it with speed, intelligence, and vision. Another Spanish star, Iniesta became a fixture with the Barcelona team starting with his first appearance in 2002. Small but fast, Iniesta partnered with Xavi for years to make Barcelona tick. His quick, accurate passing and agile movement help unlock defenses. Iniesta has provided critical goals, too. He netted a crucial extra-time winner against Chelsea in the 2009 Champions League semifinals. Barcelona went on to win its third European Cup that year with Iniesta playing a key role in the final against Manchester United.

FAST FACT

Six FC Barcelona players have won the Ballon d'Or, which has been awarded to the best player in Europe or the world over the years. Those players are Luis Suárez (1960); Johan Cruyff (1973 and 1974); Hristo Stoichkov (1994); Rivaldo (1999); Ronaldinho (2005); and Lionel Messi (2009, 2010, 2011, 2012, and 2015).

Neymar da Silva Santos Júnior, known by just his first name, is the latest in a line of world-beating Brazilians to wear the Barcelona jersey. He was already a top player in South America when he joined the club in 2013. Neymar wows fans with his speed and his clever dribbling. The flamboyant attacker also can fill the net. In 2014–15, his second year with Barcelona, Neymar scored 43 goals, second only to Messi.

FC BARCELONA TEAM FILE

NAME: Futbol Club Barcelona

YEAR FOUNDED: 1899

WHERE THEY PLAY: Camp Nou, Barcelona, Spain

LA LIGA TITLES: 24 (most recent in 2015–16)

COPAS DEL REY: 29 (most recent in 2016–17)

EUROPEAN CUP/CHAMPIONS LEAGUE TITLES: 5 (most recent in 2014–15)

KEY RECORDS

- Most career goals: Lionel Messi, 541 through the 2016–17 season
- Most appearances: Xavi, 869 games

AUTHOR'S DREAM TEAM

GOALKEEPER: Antoni Ramallets

DEFENSE: Carles Puyol, Ronald Koeman, Joan Segarra

MIDFIELD: Xavi, Pep Guardiola, Andres Iniesta, Johan Cruyff

FORWARDS: Ronaldinho, Laszlo Kubala, Lionel Messi

TIMELINE

1899

Swiss businessman Hans Gamper places a newspaper advertisement and gathers a group of soccer players to form Futbol Club Barcelona.

1929

FC Barcelona wins the first season of the new Spanish soccer league, La Liga, finishing two points ahead of Real Madrid.

1952

Barcelona wins five competitions, including La Liga and the Copa del Rey.

1957

Barcelona moves into Camp Nou, its new, 93,000-seat stadium. It remains the club's home today.

1973

Johan Cruyff joins the team. He leads Barcelona to a 22-game unbeaten streak, a 5–0 win over rival Real Madrid, and the club's first league championship in 14 years.

1992

Barcelona finally wins its first European Cup with a 1–0 win in extra time over Sampdoria.

1994

Under now-manager Johan Cruyff, Barcelona wins its fourth consecutive league title for the first time since the 1950s.

2009

Manager Pep Guardiola leads the club to a La Liga title, the Copa del Rey, and its third Champions League title.

2011

After defeating rival Real Madrid in the Champions League semifinals, Barcelona defeats Manchester United for its fourth European title.

2015

FC Barcelona conquers Europe again. A 3–1 win over Juventus marks the club's fifth European title and its third in six years.

GLOSSARY

academy

A system for professional clubs that helps develop young players.

civil war

A war between opposing groups of citizens from the same country fighting for control of its government.

debut

First appearance.

dictator

A ruler with total power over a country.

extra time

Two 15-minute overtime periods played if the score is tied at the end of 90 minutes plus stoppage time.

flamboyant

Exuberant, confident, flashy.

forward

A player positioned closest to the goal, ahead of most of his or her teammates.

garnet

A shade of deep red.

penalty area

The box in front of the goal where a player is granted a penalty kick if he or she is fouled.

refugee

A person who has been forced to leave his or her country in order to escape war, persecution, or natural disaster.

set pieces

Plays such as corner kicks, free kicks, and throw-ins that put the ball back into play after a stoppage.

FOR MORE INFORMATION

BOOKS

Crisfield, Deborah. *The Everything Kids' Soccer Book: Rules, Techniques, and More about Your Favorite Sport!* Avon, MA: Adams Media, 2015.

Jökulsson, Illugi. *Messi*. New York: Abbeville, 2015.

Jökulsson, Illugi. *Neymar: The New Pelé*. New York: Abbeville, 2015.

WEBSITES

To learn more about FC Barcelona, visit abdobooklinks.com. These links are routinely monitored and updated to provide the most current information available.

PLACE TO VISIT

CAMP NOU AND FC BARCELONA MUSEUM

Camp Nou, C. Aristides Maillol, s/n, 08028 Barcelona, Spain
Phone: + 34 902 18 99 00
fcbarcelona.com/tour/buy-tickets

Experience the history of FC Barcelona and what makes it *més que un club* at the FC Barcelona Museum. Located at the famous Camp Nou in Barcelona, visitors can also buy tickets to tour the home stadium of FC Barcelona.

INDEX

ABOUT THE AUTHOR

Jonathan Avise is a reporter, writer, and digital media editor from Minneapolis, Minnesota. An avid soccer fan, he is a die-hard supporter of north London's Tottenham Hotspur.